rld

Once a year, on a
warm summer night
when the moon is full,
all toys everywhere
leave their owners for
a night of fun.

Bear, Rabbit, Mimi and Peep felt very excited.

'I haven't done this before,' said Bear.

'Nor have we,' said Mimi and Peep.

'Well, I have,' said Rabbit, 'and it's great!'

'Here we are,' said
Rabbit.
'What is it?' asked
Peep.
'Looks like a very big
step,' said Bear.
They climbed up.

'Oh, look, another one,' said Mimi. 'Yes,' said Rabbit, 'there are many more, and when we have climbed them all we will be on top of the world!'

Up and up they climbed...

and up some more...

until, at last, as night became day, they found themselves on top of the world!

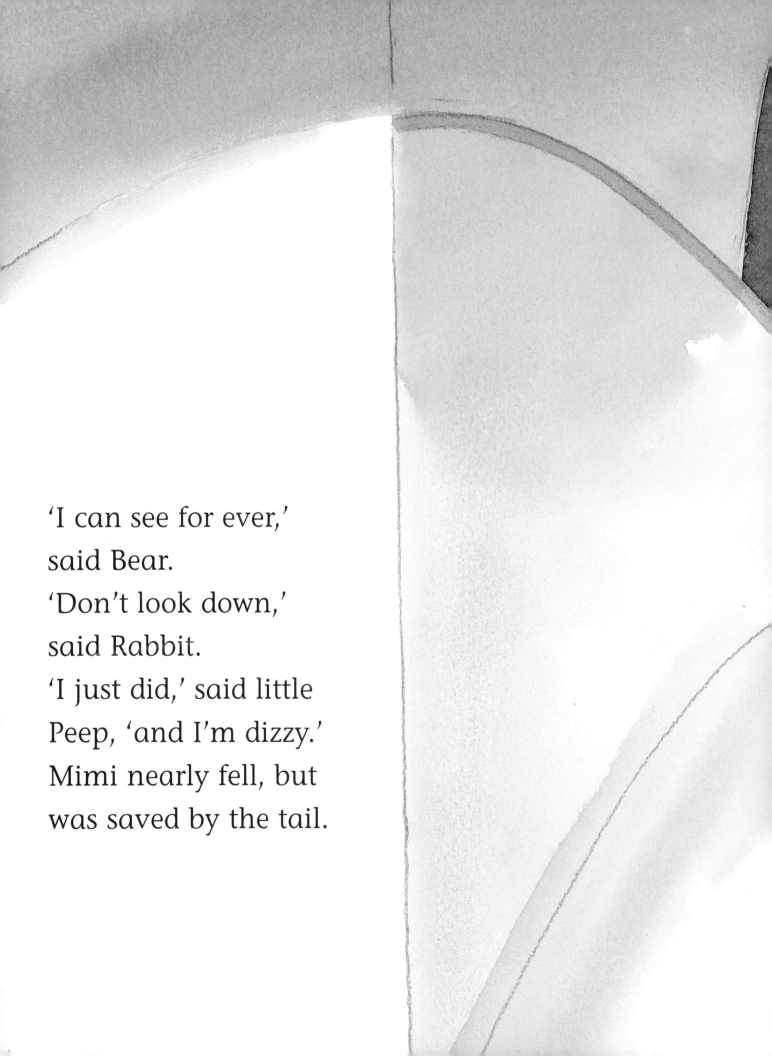

'I can see for ever,'
said Bear.
'Don't look down,'
said Rabbit.
'I just did,' said little
Peep, 'and I'm dizzy.'
Mimi nearly fell, but
was saved by the tail.

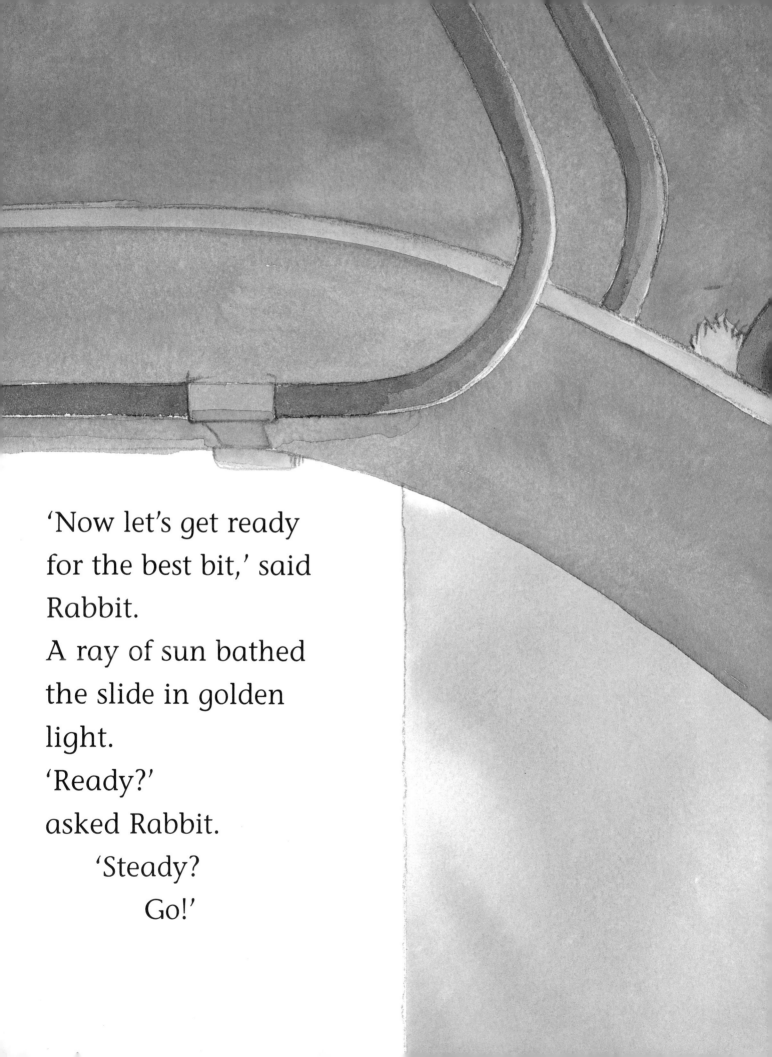

'Now let's get ready
for the best bit,' said
Rabbit.
A ray of sun bathed
the slide in golden
light.
'Ready?'
asked Rabbit.
     'Steady?
         Go!'

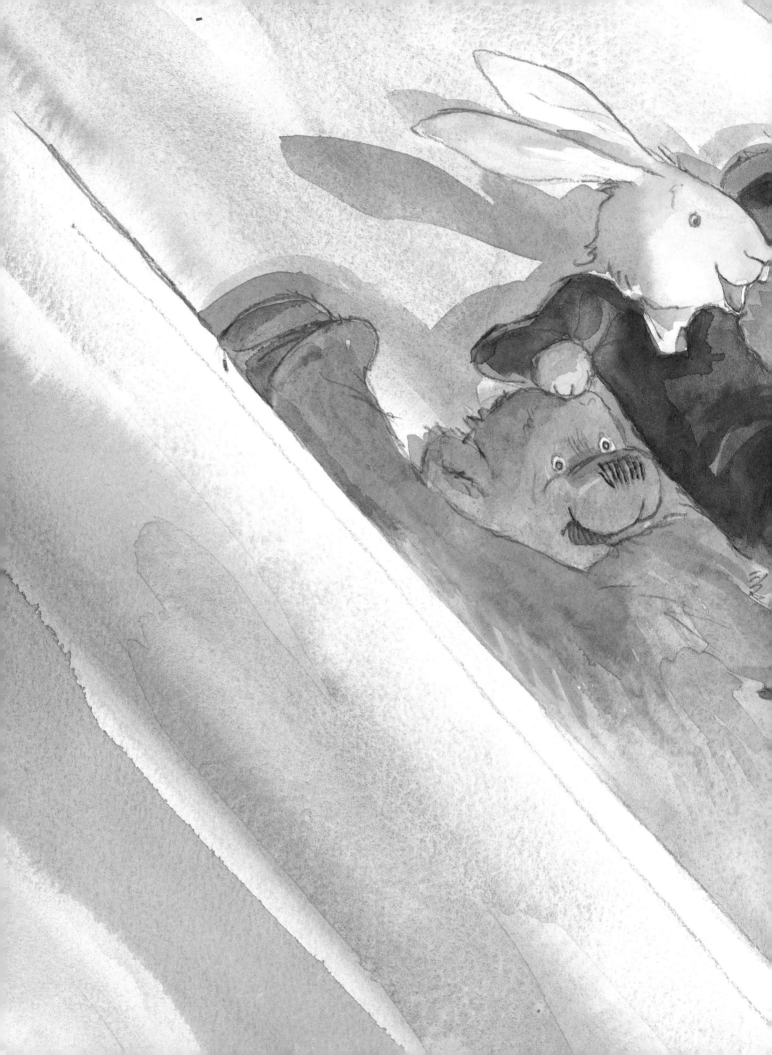

'Wow!' said Peep.
'Let's do it again.'
But there was no
time left.
Perhaps next year,
one warm,
moonlit
night....